easy **UKULELE TAB EDITION**

UKE 'AN PLAY
THE WH[O]

Produced by
Alfred Music
P.O. Box 10003
Van Nuys, CA 91410-0003
alfred.com

ISBN-10: 1-4706-1792-7
ISBN-13: 978-1-4706-1792-9

Cover photo used by permission

 Alfred Cares. Contents printed on environmentally responsible paper.

CONTENTS

BARGAIN

Tune down 1/2 step to match recording:
④ = G♭ ② = E♭
③ = C♭ ① = A♭

Words and Music by
PETER TOWNSHEND

Moderately fast ♩ = 132

Intro:

B7sus

B7

B7sus

B7

1. I'd

𝄋 *Verses 1, 2 & 3:*

B

G D E

B

glad - ly   lose__ me to find__ you.   I'd glad - ly give up all__ I have.__
(2.3.) glad - ly   lose__ me to find__ you.   'n' glad - ly give up all__ I've got.__

G D E

B

D

To find   you,   I'd suf - fer an - y - thing__ and be glad.__
To catch   you,   I'm gon - na run and__ nev - er   stop.__

Bargain - 5 - 1

4

Bargain - 5 - 2

6

Cont. in notation

you._____

D.S. % al Coda

3. I'd

The best I ev - er had.__

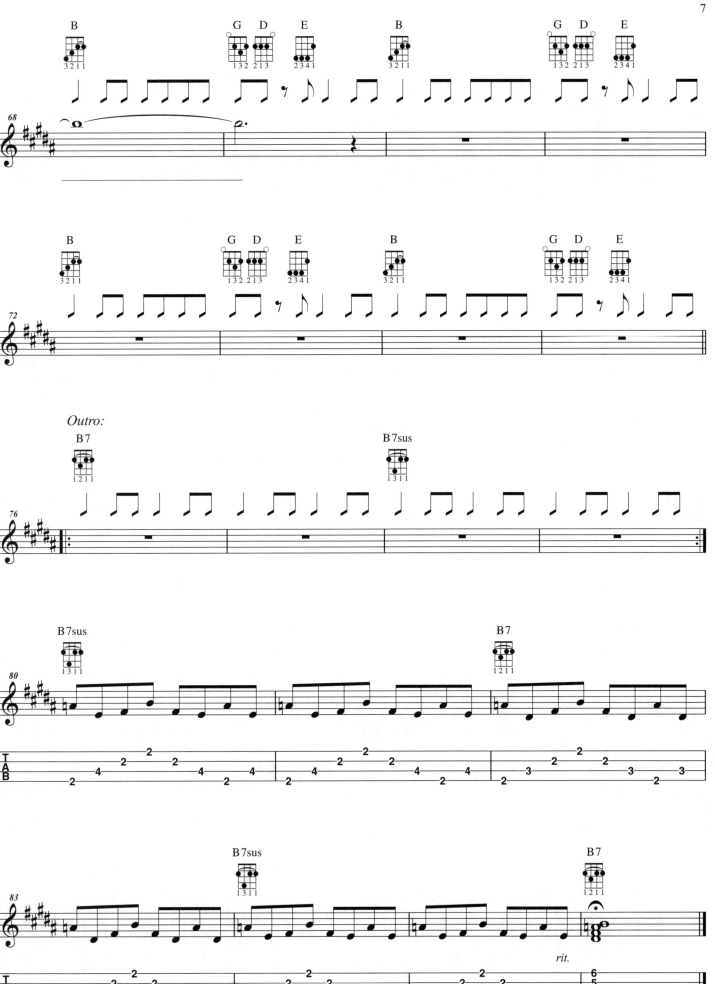

Outro:

BEHIND BLUE EYES

Words and Music by
PETER TOWNSHEND

12

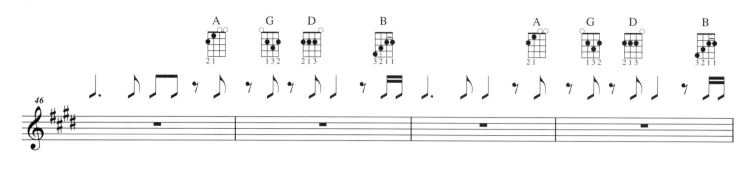

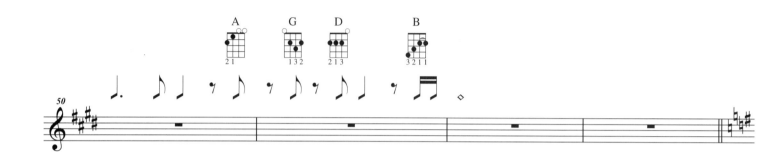

Half-time ♩ = 60

Outro:

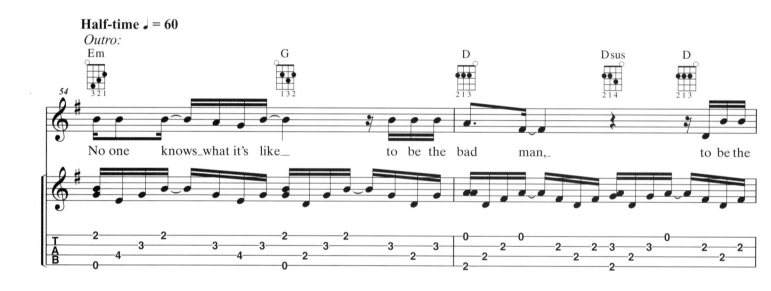

No one knows what it's like to be the bad man, to be the

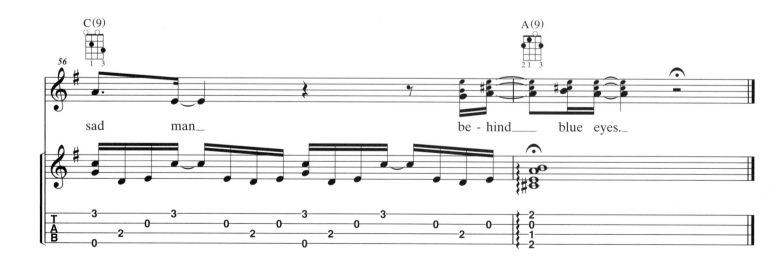

sad man be - hind blue eyes.

I CAN SEE FOR MILES

Words and Music by
PETER TOWNSHEND

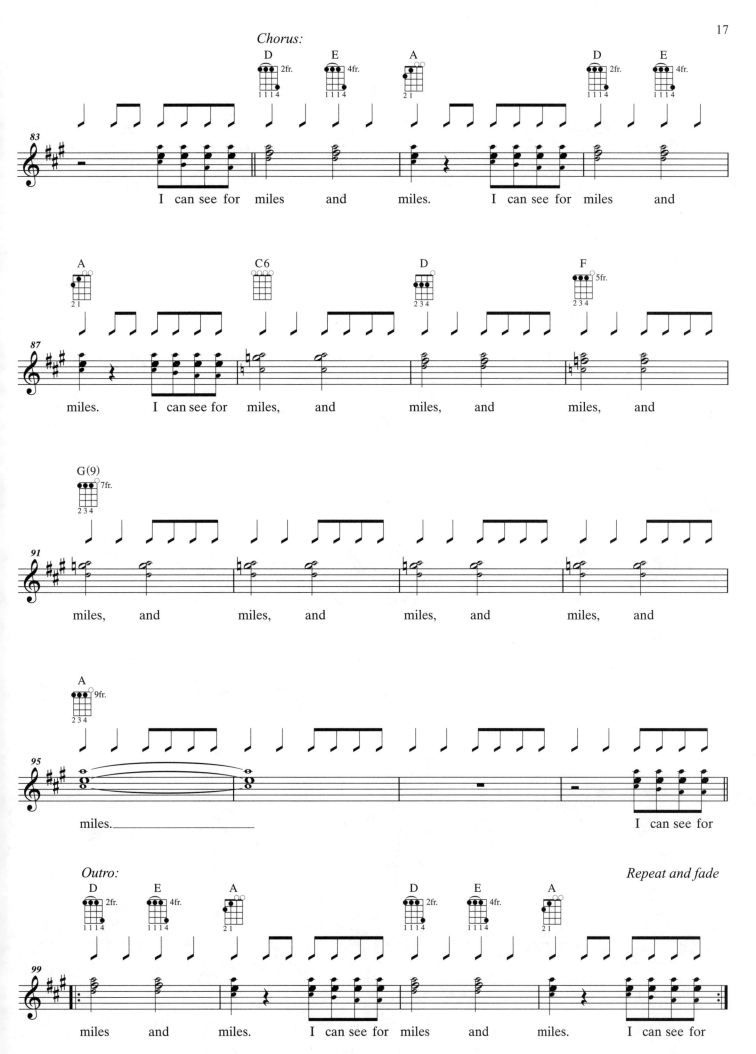

I CAN'T EXPLAIN

Moderately fast ♩ = 140

Words and Music by
PETER TOWNSHEND

20

♦ *Coda*

Resume intro fig. simile

can't ex - plain.__ (Can't ex - plain.__)For-give me one more time,__ now. (Can't ex - plain.__)

Instrumental:

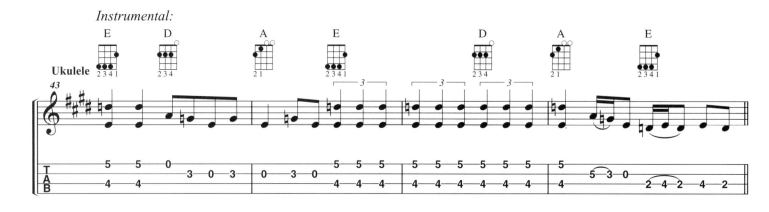

Ukulele

Chorus:

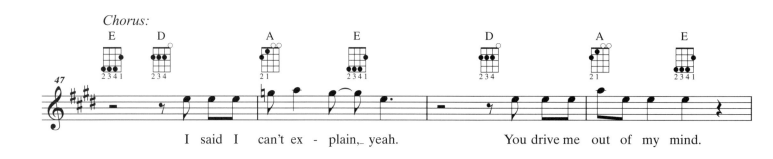

I said I can't ex - plain,__ yeah. You drive me out of my mind.

Ukulele

Yeah, I'm the wor-ry-ing kind,__ babe. I said I can't ex - plain.__

I'M FREE

Words and Music by
PETER TOWNSHEND

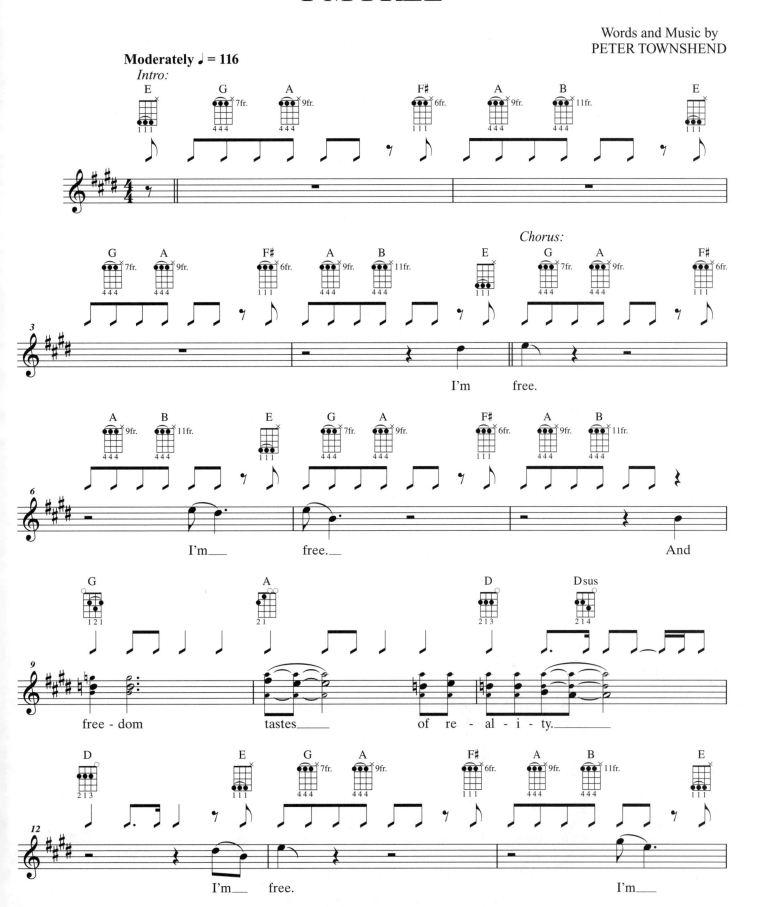

I'm Free - 3 - 1

22

I'm Free - 3 - 2

THE KIDS ARE ALRIGHT

Words and Music by
PETER TOWNSHEND

The Kids Are Alright - 5 - 2

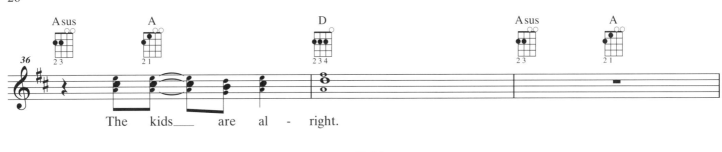

The kids____ are al - right.

Bridge:

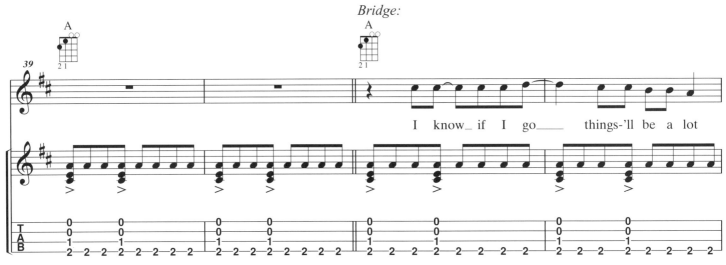

I know_ if I go____ things-'ll be a lot

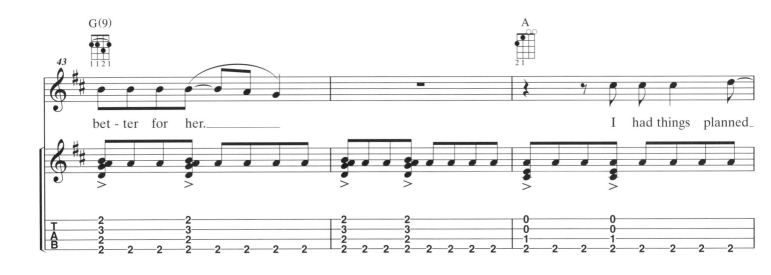

bet - ter for her._____ I had things planned_

____ but her folks would-n't let her._____ 3. I don't

28

The Kids Are Alright - 5 - 5

MAGIC BUS

Words and Music by
PETER TOWNSHEND

Ev-'ry day__ I get in the queue,__ to get on the bus that takes__ me to you.

Magic Bus - 5 - 1

I don't care how much__ I pay,__ I wan-na

drive my bus to my ba-by each day.__

I want it. I want it. I want it. I want it. I (You

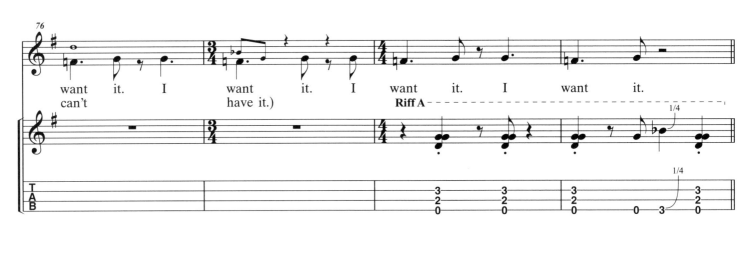

Verse 3:

(Mag-ic bus._)

I said, now I've got my mag-ic bus._ I said,

now I've got my mag - ic bus.__ I

drive my ba - by ev - er - y way, each

time I go a dif - f'rent way.__ I

want it. I want it. I want it. I want it. I

MY GENERATION

Words and Music by
PETER TOWNSHEND

Moderately fast ♩ = 188 (♫ = ♩♪)

Intro:

*Original recording sounds one step lower than written.

Verses 1 & 2:

Rhy. Fig. 1

end Rhy. Fig. 1

1. Peo-ple try to put us d-down, (Talk-in' 'bout my gen - er - a - tion.)
2. *See additional lyrics*

w/Rhy. Fig. 1, *3 times*

just be-cause we get a-round. (Talk-in' 'bout my gen - er - a - tion.)

Things they do look aw - ful c-cold, (Talk-in' 'bout my gen - er - a - tion.)

hope I die be-fore___ I get old. This is my___ gen - er - a - tion.
(Talk-in' 'bout my gen - er - a - tion.)

My Generation - 5 - 1

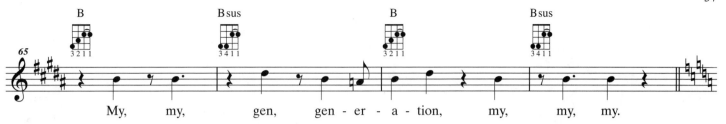

My, my, gen, gen - er - a - tion, my, my, my.

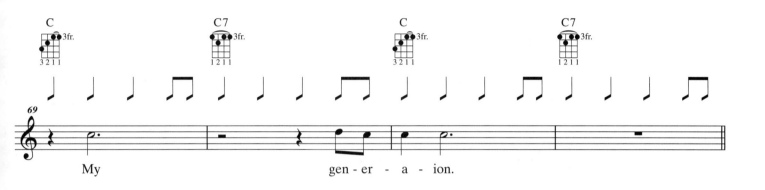

My gen - er - a - ion.

Verse 4:

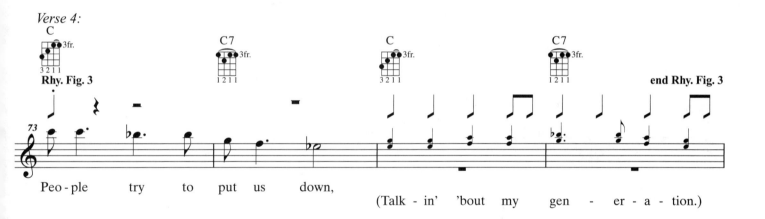

Peo - ple try to put us down, (Talk - in' 'bout my gen - er - a - tion.)

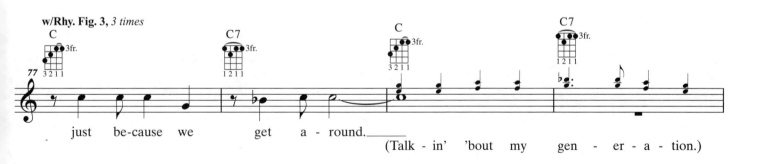

just be-cause we get a - round._____ (Talk - in' 'bout my gen - er - a - tion.)

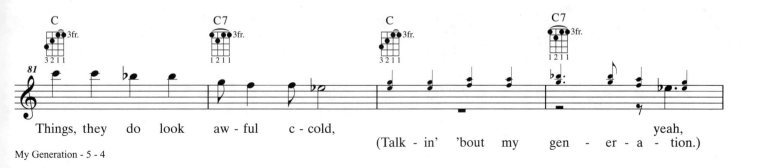

Things, they do look aw - ful c - cold, yeah, (Talk - in' 'bout my gen - er - a - tion.)

My Generation - 5 - 4

38

Verse 2:
Why don't you all fade away?
And don't try to dig what we all say.
I'm not tryin' to cause a big sensation,
I'm just talkin' about my generation.
My generation, this is my generation, baby.
(To Interlude:)

PINBALL WIZARD

Words and Music by
PETER TOWNSHEND

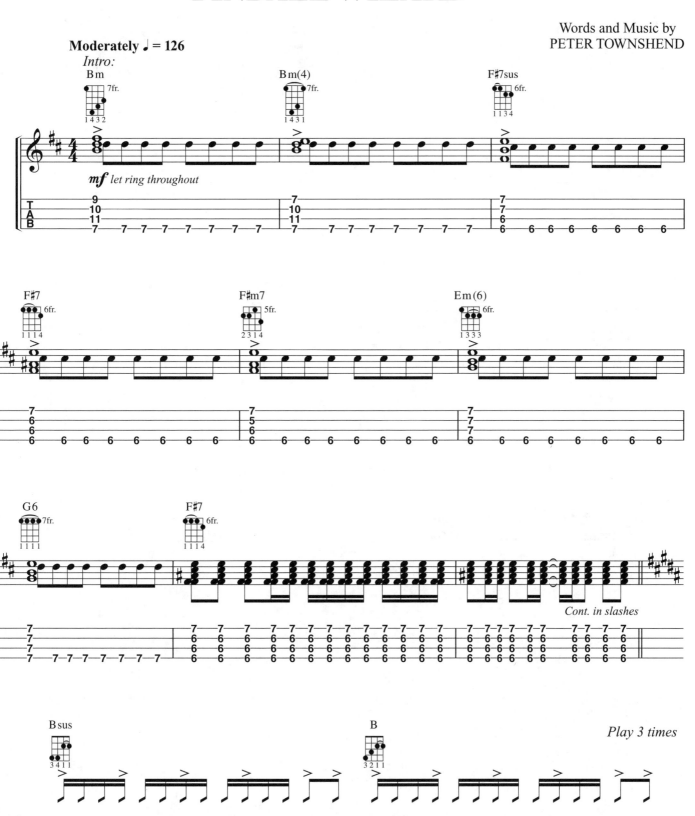

Pinball Wizard - 5 - 1

42

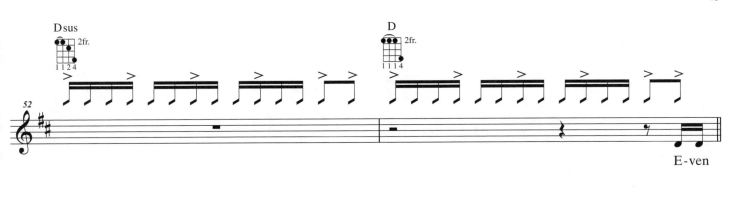

E-ven

Verse 4:

on my fa-v'rite ta - ble, he can beat my best. His di - sci - ples lead him in___ and

he just does the rest.___ He's got cra - zy lit-tle fin - gers, nev - er seen him fall.___ That

Ukulele

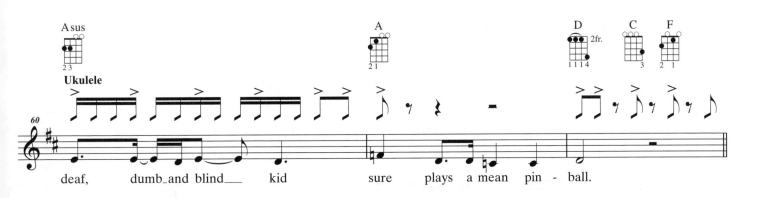

deaf, dumb_and blind___ kid sure plays a mean pin - ball.

Outro:

Repeat and fade

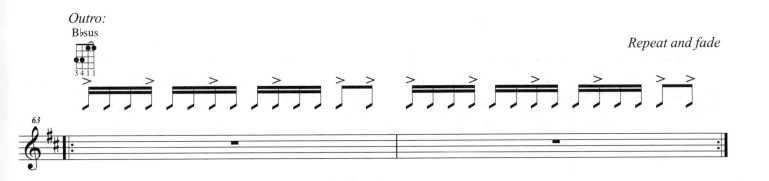

THE REAL ME

Moderately fast ♩ = 146

Words and Music by
PETER TOWNSHEND

The Real Me - 4 - 1

46

The Real Me - 4 - 3

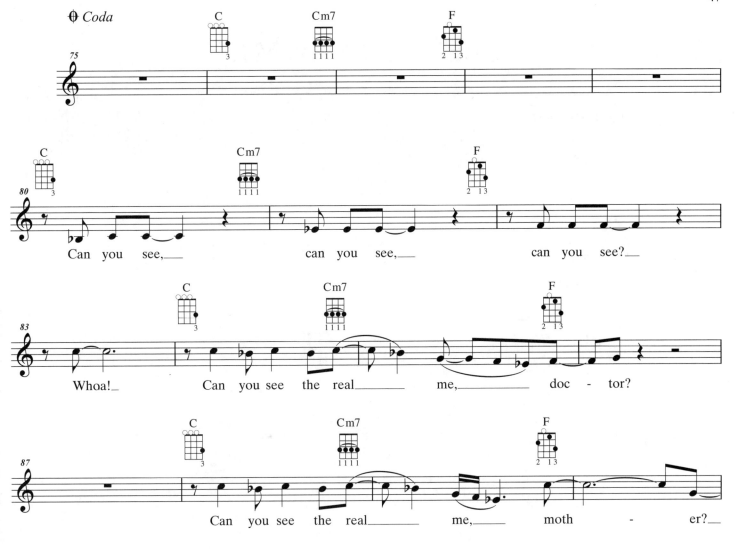

⊕ *Coda*

Can you see,___ can you see,___ can you see?___

Whoa!_ Can you see the real___ me,___ doc - tor?

Can you see the real___ me,___ moth - er?___

Uke tacet

___ Can you see___ the real me? (Me, me, me, me, me, me.)

Verse 2:
I went back to my mother, I said, "I'm crazy, ma, help me."
She said, "I know how it feels, son, 'cause it runs in the family."

Chorus 2:
Can you see the real me, mother, mother?
Can you see the real me, mother?
Whoa, mother.
Can you see, can you see the real me?
Can you see, can you see the real me, the real me, the real me?
(To Verse 3:)

Chorus 3:
Can you see the real me, preacher, preacher?
Can you see the real me, preacher?
(To Coda)

The Real Me - 4 - 4

SEE ME, FEEL ME

Words and Music by
PETER TOWNSHEND

See Me, Feel Me - 4 - 1

See Me, Feel Me - 4 - 2

50

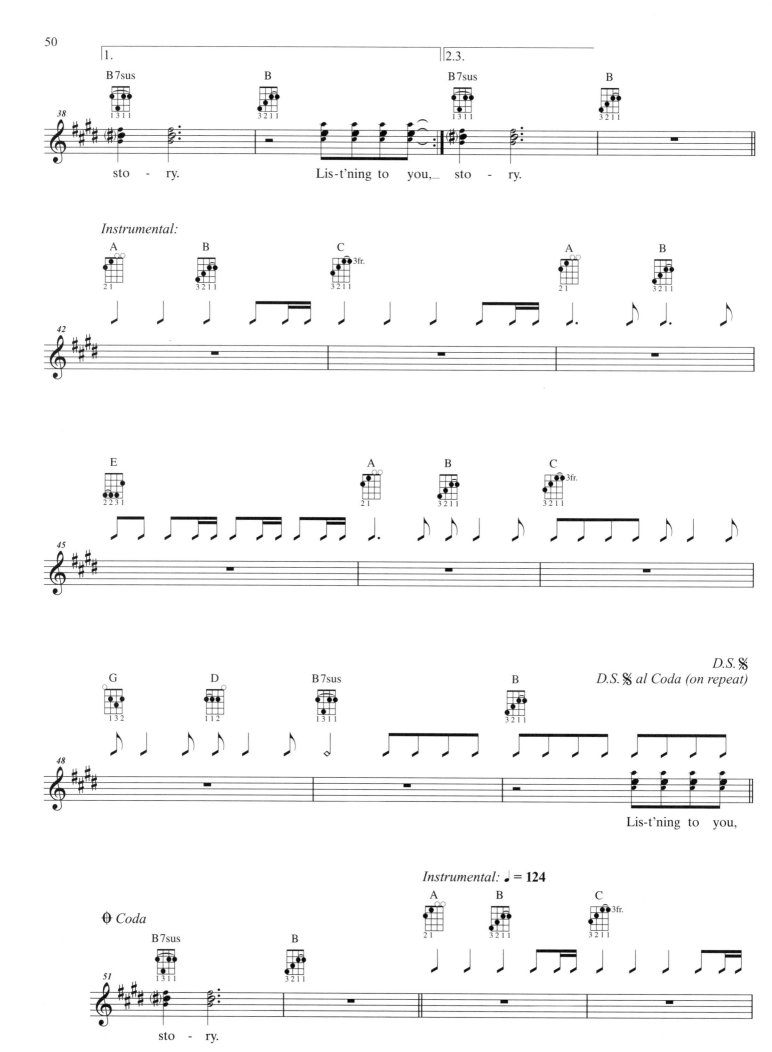

See Me, Feel Me - 4 - 4

WHO ARE YOU

Words and Music by
PETER TOWNSHEND

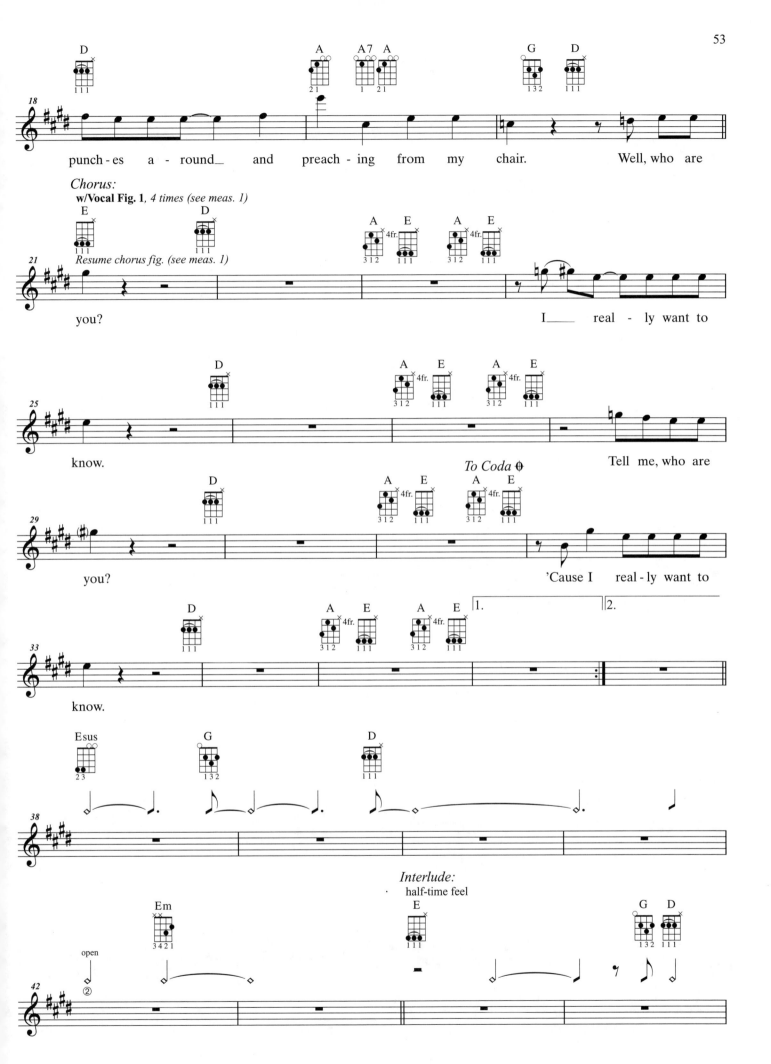

54

57

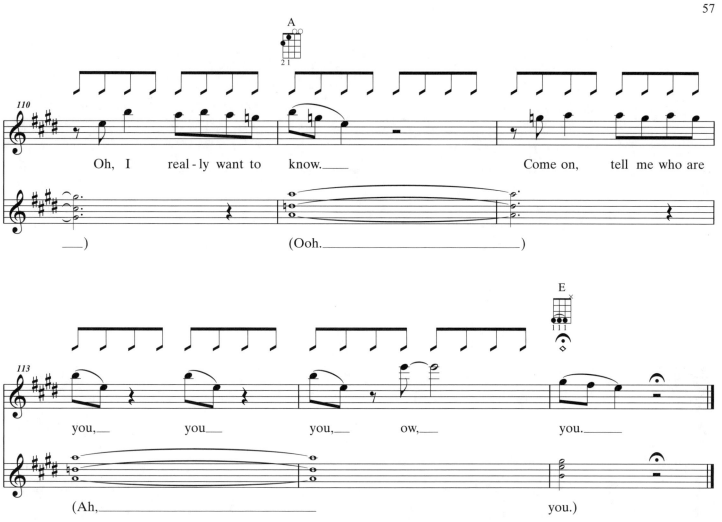

Oh, I real-ly want to know.___ Come on, tell me who are

___) (Ooh.___)

you,___ you___ you,___ ow,___ you.___

(Ah,___ you.)

Verse 2:
I took the tube back out of town, back to the rolling pin.
I felt a little like a dying clown with a streak of "Rin Tin Tin."
I stretched back and I hiccupped, and looked back on my busy day.
Eleven hours in the tin pan, God, there's got to be another way.

Chorus 2 & 3:
Well, who are you?
Oh, who are you?
Come on, tell me who are you?
Oh, who the f*** are you?

Verse 3:
I know there's a place you walked where love falls from the trees.
My heart is like a broken cup, I only feel right on my knees.
I spill out like a sewer hole and still receive your kiss.
How can I measure up to anyone now after such a love as this?
(To Chorus 3:)

Who Are You - 6 - 6

WON'T GET FOOLED AGAIN

Words and Music by
PETER TOWNSHEND

Moderately fast ♩ = 132

we don't get fooled___ a - gain.___

No, no!

Instrumental:

I'll

Bridge:

move___ my - self and my fam - 'ly a - side,___

Cont. rhy. simile

if we hap-pen to be left half___ a - live.___ I'll get all my pa-pers and smile___

___ at the sky, oh, I know that the hyp - no - tized nev - er lie.

SQUEEZE BOX

Moderately fast ♩ = 132
Intro:

Words and Music by
PETER TOWNSHEND

Squeeze Box - 3 - 1

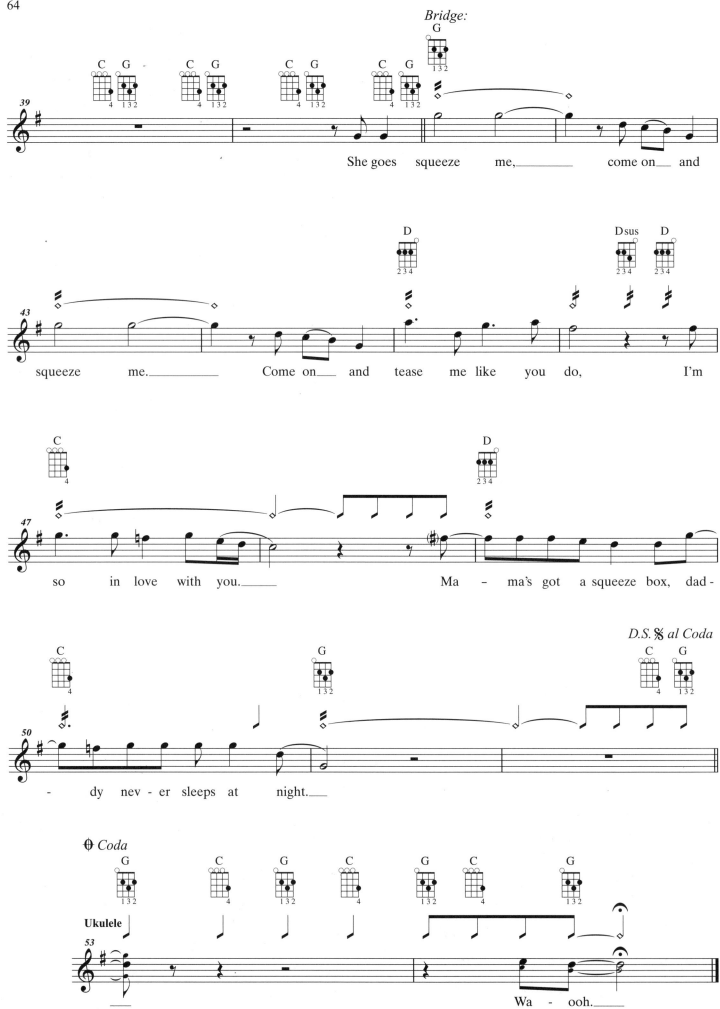